Dear Parents and Educators,

Welcome to Penguin Young Readers! As parents and educators, you know that each child develops at his or her own pace—in terms of speech, critical thinking, and, of course, reading. Penguin Young Readers recognizes this fact. As a result, each Penguin Young Readers book is assigned a traditional easy-to-read level (1–4) as well as a Guided Reading Level (A–P). Both of these systems will help you choose the right book for your child. Please refer to the back of each book for specific leveling information. Penguin Young Readers features esteemed authors and illustrators, stories about favorite characters, fascinating nonfiction, and more!

Woodward and McTwee

LEVEL **2**

GUIDED READING LEVEL **I**

This book is perfect for a **Progressing Reader** who:
- can figure out unknown words by using picture and context clues;
- can recognize beginning, middle, and ending sounds;
- can make and confirm predictions about what will happen in the text; and
- can distinguish between fiction and nonfiction.

Here are some **activities** you can do during and after reading this book:
- Picture Clues: Use the pictures to tell the story. Have the child go through the book, retelling the story just by looking at the pictures.
- Homophones: Homophones are words that sound alike but have different meanings. In this book, the words *here* and *hear* are homophones. Think of homophones for these other words from the book: *right, one, would, not*. Then, on a separate sheet of paper, write down each pair of homophones and a sentence that includes both words.

Remember, sharing the love of reading with a child is the best gift you can give!

—Bonnie Bader, EdM
  Penguin Young Readers program

*Penguin Young Readers are leveled by independent reviewers applying the standards developed by Irene Fountas and Gay Su Pinnell in *Matching Books to Readers: Using Leveled Books in Guided Reading*, Heinemann, 1999.

For Pendy and Coco—JF

PENGUIN YOUNG READERS
Published by the Penguin Group
Penguin Group (USA) LLC, 375 Hudson Street, New York, New York 10014, USA

USA | Canada | UK | Ireland | Australia | New Zealand | India | South Africa | China

penguin.com
A Penguin Random House Company

Copyright © 2014 by Jonathan Fenske. All rights reserved. Published in 2014 by Penguin Young Readers, an imprint of Penguin Group (USA) LLC, 345 Hudson Street, New York, New York 10014. Manufactured in China.

Library of Congress Cataloging-in-Publication Data is available.

ISBN 978-0-448-47991-0 (pbk)   10 9 8 7 6 5 4 3 2 1
ISBN 978-0-448-47992-7 (hc)   10 9 8 7 6 5 4 3 2 1

Penguin Young Readers
An Imprint of Penguin Group (USA) LLC

by Jonathan Fenske

WOODWARD
AND McTWEE

PENGUIN YOUNG READERS

LEVEL

2

PROGRESSING
READER

THE REALLY SILLY HIPPO

Hey, Woodward.

Guess what?

What, McTwee?

I hear there is
a really silly
hippopotamus
wandering
around this book.

Really?

Yep. Want to
try to find
him?

YES!

Is he up

high?

No.

CREAK

CREAK

Is he down low?

Uh-uh.

No.

Is he in the back?

No.

Is he in the front?

No.

Is he on the right?

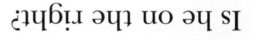

No.

Is he on the left?

Well, it seems like the only hippopotamus wandering around this book is ME.

WHISTLE

Hmmm . . . I think
I have been tricked.

Boy, do I
feel silly.

HAR!
HAR!
HA!
HA!
HEE!
HEE!

Really?

Har! Har!

Wow. He really fell for that one!

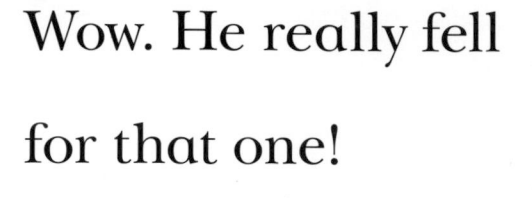

He never even saw it coming.

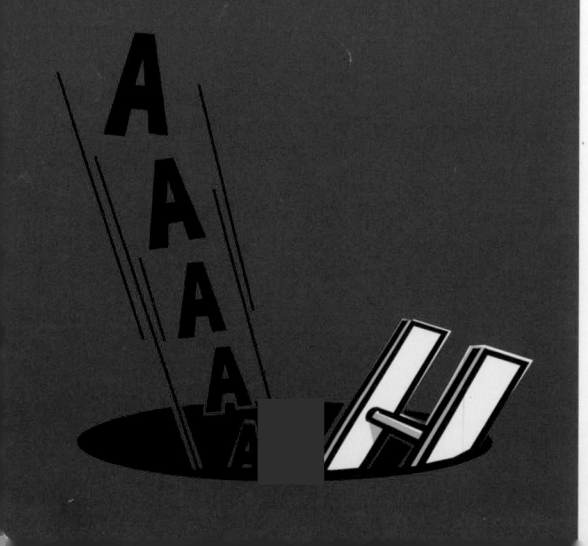

Hey, McTwee. I hear there is a really silly bird wandering around this book.

That would be me.

HIDE-AND-SEEK

Hi, McTwee. Do you want to play
hide-and-seek?

Sure, Woodward.

This should be fun.

This is so exciting!

1 . . . 2 . . . 3 . . .

4 . . . 5 . . . 6 . . . 7 . . . 8 . . . 9 . . . 10.

Ready or not, here I come!

You are behind that tree.

That was too fast.

May I please try again?

Behind the

Behind the

trash can.

slide.

Behind the

Behind the

birdbath.

bench.

I give up.

You hide, and I

will seek.

I will show him

how it is done.

1, 2, 3, 4, 5, 6, 7,

8, 9, 10.

Ready or not,

here I come!

Ha-ha!

Oh, McTwee,

where are you?

Tee-hee!

Uh-oh.

SPLAT!

He is not behind the trash can.

He is not behind the slide.

He is not behind the birdbath.

He is not behind the bench.

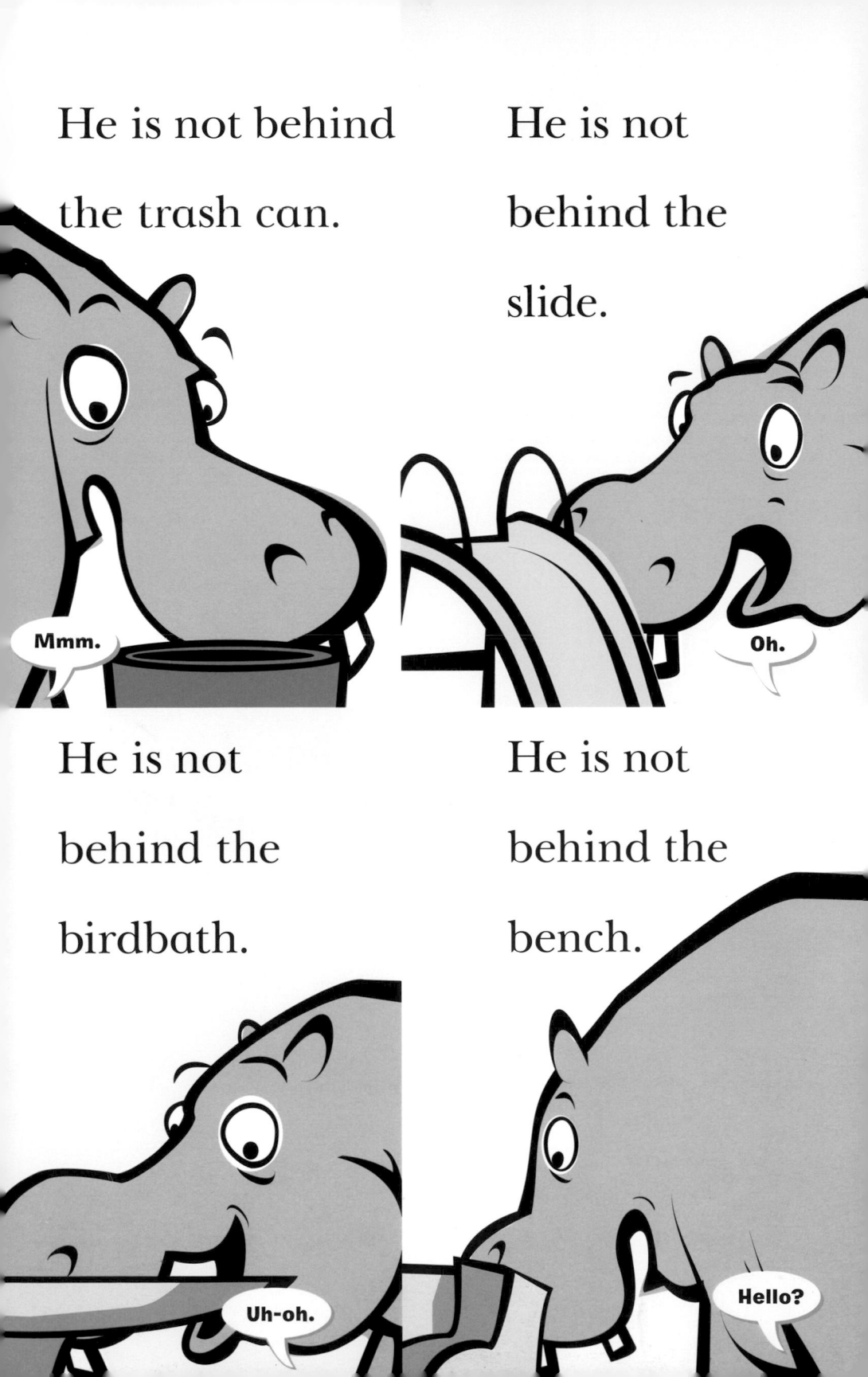

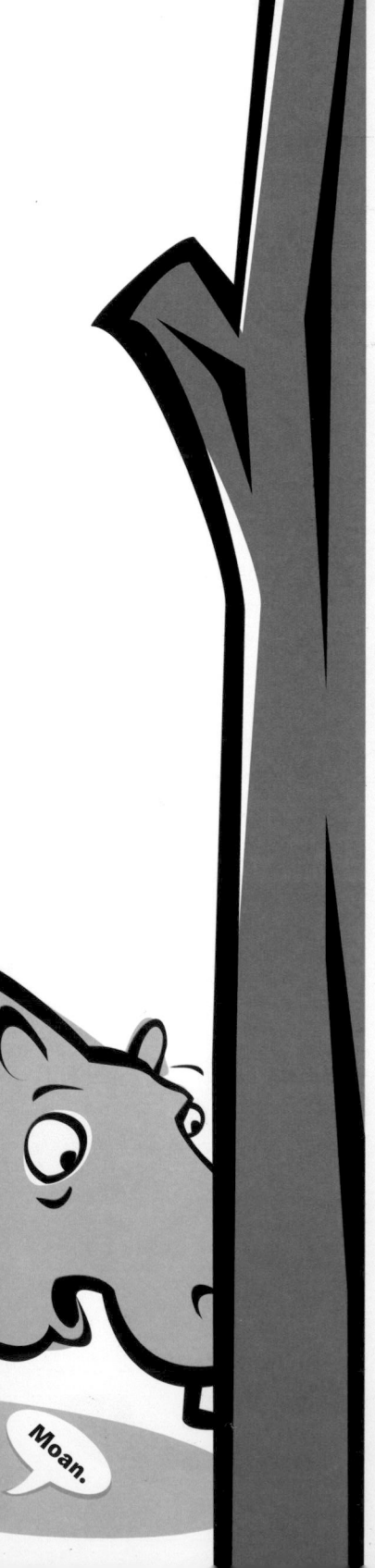

And he is
not behind
the tree.
He has to
be around
here
somewhere.

Groan!

Moan.

Do you hear

something?

There you are, you sneaky

little bird!

Does anybody have a spatula?